DUDLEY PUBLIC LIBRARIES

The loan of this book may be renewed if not required by other
readers, by contacting the library from which it was borrowed.

How the
Camel
Got His Hump

Retold by Robert James

Illustrated by Stefania Colnaghi

FRANKLIN WATTS
LONDON•SYDNEY

First published in 2010 by
Franklin Watts
338 Euston Road
London
NW1 3BH

Franklin Watts Australia
Level 17/207 Kent Street
Sydney
NSW 2000

Text © Franklin Watts 2010
Illustration © Stefania Colnaghi 2010

The rights of Robert James to be identified as the
author and Stefania Colnaghi as the illustrator of this Work
have been asserted in accordance with the Copyright,
Designs and Patents Act, 1988.

A CIP catalogue record for this book is available
from the British Library.

ISBN 978 0 7496 9405 0 (hbk)
ISBN 978 0 7496 9411 1 (pbk)

Series Editor: Jackie Hamley
Series Advisor: Catherine Glavina
Series Designer: Peter Scoulding

Printed in China

Franklin Watts is a division of
Hachette Children's Books,
an Hachette UK company.
www.hachette.co.uk

This Just So story is
based on a tale written
by an author called
Rudyard Kipling over
a hundred years ago.

Just So stories give fun
ideas for why different
animals are like they are.

Long ago, when the world was new, there was much work to do.

The animals worked hard, but Camel was lazy.

The desert god
saw this.

"Why are you so lazy, Camel?" he asked.

"Humph!"
said Camel.

8

"You're very rude,"
said the desert god.

"Humph!" said Camel.

With that, the desert god cast a spell.

Camel's back puffed up.

"Now you will work!"
said the desert god.

"How can I work with this on my back?" cried Camel.

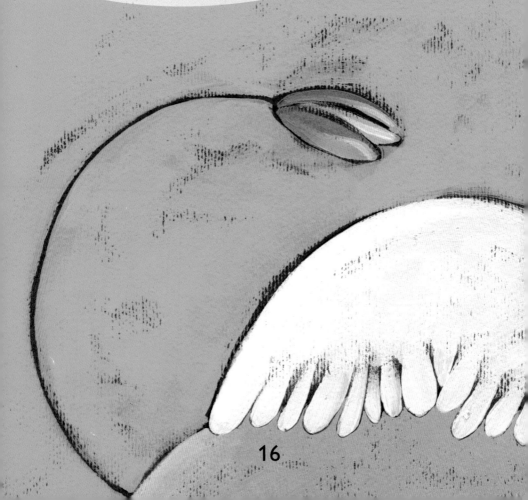

16

17

"With that on your back, you can work for days without eating or drinking!" said the desert god.

And that's how Camel
got his humph, or hump
as we call it today.

20

Puzzle Time!

a

b

c

d

e

f

Put these pictures in the right order and tell the story!

rude

annoyed

lazy

cross

Which words describe Camel and
which describe the desert god?

Turn over for answers!

Notes for adults

TADPOLES are structured to provide support for newly independent readers. The stories may also be used by adults for sharing with young children.

Starting to read alone can be daunting. **TADPOLES** help by providing visual support and repeating words and phrases. These books will both develop confidence and encourage reading and rereading for pleasure.

If you are reading this book with a child, here are a few suggestions:

1. Make reading fun! Choose a time to read when you and the child are relaxed and have time to share the story.
2. Talk about the story before you start reading. Look at the cover and the blurb. What might the story be about? Why might the child like it?
3. Encourage the child to retell the story, using the jumbled picture puzzle as a starting point. Extend vocabulary with the matching words to characters puzzle.
4. Talk about how the story has fun with how different animals look, and see if you can think of other animals and why they might look the way they do.
5. Give praise! Remember that small mistakes need not always be corrected.

Answers

Here is the correct order:

1. d 2. e 3. a 4. b 5. f 6. c

Words to describe Camel:
lazy, rude

Words to describe
the desert god:
annoyed, cross